The SUPER SWOOPER DINOSAUR

For Arthur and Edith—M.W.

For Harry and Max—L.L.

An Imprint of Sterling Publishing
387 Park Avenue South
New York, NY 10016

First published in Great Britain in 2012 by Orchard Books, a imprint of Hachette Children's Books.

Text © 2012 by Martin Waddell

Illustrations © 2012 by Leonie Lord

This 2013 edition published by Sandy Creek.

Designed by Sophie Stericker

ISBN 978-1-4351-5000-3

Manufactured in China

Lot #:

2 4 6 8 10 9 7 5 3 1

09/13

The SUPER SWOOPER DINOSAUR

Martin Waddell & Leonie Lord

Sandy Creek
NEW YORK

One day, Hal and his little dog, Billy, were
out playing when the sky darkened and . . .

A SUPER SWOOPER DINOSAUR

landed in Hal's garden.

KER-PLUMP!

"Can I play with you?" he asked Hal and Billy.

"Yes, please!" said Hal. "What games will we play?"

"Hide-and-seek!" suggested the super swooper.

So, they played hide-and-seek.
The super swooper was so excited he
got himself into a flap!

100!

99...

98...

"Here I come . . ." called Hal.

"Maybe you're a bit too big for hide-and-seek," said Hal.

"Perhaps we should try something else," Hal suggested.

"How about dino dancing?"
said the super swooper.

The super swooper swooped up onto the roof of Hal's house and danced on the tiles.

"You can't dino dance on the roof!" said Hal.

Hal had to
do something,

so . . .

"Last one in the paddling pool is a BLUE BANANA!" shouted Hal.

Hal raced outside but . . .

"**Look out below!**"

cried the super swooper,
swooping down towards the
paddling pool.

Hal's mom got SOAKED!

"Oh, Mom! We're so sorry!" said Hal.

But Hal's mom was cranky. "Your games are too rough and rowdy," she scolded the super swooper. "If you can't play nicely with Hal, you'd better go home!"

The super swooper was VERY upset.

His bottom lip wibbled and wobbled and he started to sob.

"Please, Mom,
let him stay.
We're his best
friends," said Hal.

"He has no one to play
with but us.
COME ON, MOM,
PLEASE?"
pleaded Hal.

"Oh, all right . . . he can stay,"
said Hal's mom.

"Thank you so much!" said the super swooper.

Then the super swooper flapped his
wings to get Mom dry.
"Thank you very much!" said Hal's mom.

And she went to get cool drinks on a tray.

"What will we play now, Hal?"

the super swooper asked.

"Hide-and-seek didn't work,
dino dancing was a disaster and
the paddling pool was a big, BIG
mistake," sighed the super swooper.

"I know what we'll do," said Hal.

"We'll do what you do best of all!"

So . . .

. . . they swooped and they swooped!
(Which is what super swooper dinosaurs do when
they're having fun with their friends.)
And it was the best game EVER!